TOWSE[

and the Haunte

Tony Ross

Andersen Press · London
Hutchinson of Australia

© 1985 by Tony Ross. First published in Great Britain in 1985 by Andersen Press Ltd., 19–21 Conway Street, London W1. Published in Australia by Hutchinson Group (Australia) Pty. Ltd., Melbourne, Victoria 3122. All rights reserved. Colour separated in Switzerland by Photolitho AG Offsetreproduktionen, Zürich. Printed in Great Britain by W. S. Cowell Ltd., Ipswich.

ISBN 0 86264 079 2

One bats-across-the-moon night, Towser was taking his stroll, when he saw Sadie, looking scared.

"Oooooooh!" moaned Towser.

"Aaaaagh!" screeched Sadie. "That's not funny. You *know* I find that old house scary. It's *haunted*."

"Nuts!" laughed Towser.

"If you're so smart," went on Sadie, "bet you daren't go in there."

"Nothing to it," muttered Towser, skipping up the steps and pushing the door open.

"No such things as ghosts," he said.

"I'll wait for you here," answered Sadie.

Once inside, creeping along a dark, creaking corridor, Towser didn't feel so brave.

Suddenly, a *horrible* face floated out of the shadows. Towser's hair and his ears stood on end. Then he saw it was only a mirror.

"Silly me!" he grinned. "There are no such things as ghosts."

A little further on, Towser stopped in his tracks. His skin crawled, his whiskers went stiff. He heard an unearthly wail.

Then he saw it was only the owl, falling past the window.

"Twit!" he growled. Then he made a rude noise.

Outside the house, Sadie was getting a little bored, when along came the King and Dr Smellie. They were taking some washing to the launderette.

"Why are you waiting here, Sadie?" asked the King. Sadie explained about Towser.

"We could have a bit of fun with these sheets," chortled the King.

Dr Smellie and the King liked the idea of playing a trick on Towser. It was usually Towser who played tricks on them.

They put on the sheets and went into the house, trying their hardest to walk like ghosts.

The King and Dr Smellie made so much noise as they giggled and stumbled up the stairs that Towser heard them coming.

Quickly, he hopped inside a cupboard, thinking that the two "ghosts" would get a fright themselves when they found that he had vanished.

From inside the cupboard Towser watched Dr Smellie glide past.

"Silly old goat has left his glasses on," he sniggered. "As if I'd think *he* was a ghost."

Then the King thumped by, waving his arms and banging his feet.

Towser could see the shape of the crown under the sheet and he could hardly stop laughing.

"As if a batty old fool in a sheet could scare *me*!"

Towser was about to get out of the cupboard, when something else floated by.

"Ooo-errr!" he gasped. "Sadie looks quite *real*."

All of a sudden, he felt he wanted to get out of the creepy old house, in spite of not believing in ghosts.

"Was it *very* scary?" asked Sadie.

"Not at all!" said Towser airily. "It was quite funny, especially when you three came in, dressed as ghosts."

"I didn't dress as a ghost," said Sadie. "You wouldn't get *me* in there!"

As Towser and Sadie made their way across the garden, the King and Dr Smellie rushed by. They were squealing, and they didn't even stop to say hello.

"Perhaps they've seen a ghost," said Sadie.

"There ain't no such thing," said Towser.

"OOOOHHH!" screeched Sadie. "What's that then?"

Something white drifted by in the moonlight.

Somewhere, something screamed.

Well . . . As Towser didn't believe in ghosts . . . he didn't wait to see.

British Library Cataloguing in Publication Data
Ross, Tony
    Towser and the haunted house.
    I. Title
    823′.914[J]   PZ7

ISBN 0-86264-079-2